The First Time

THE FIRST TIME

Erotic Fiction

Shindy Chen

Scribe

Scribe

Scribe
New York / Wyoming
Copyright ©2016 by Shindy Chen

This Scribe trade paperback edition December 2016

For information about special discounts for bulk purchases, please contact Scribe at hello@thescri.be.

Cover art designed by Francisco Reynoso.

ISBN-10: 0-9974112-6-0

ISBN-13: 978-0-9974112-6-3

See Scribe books at: www.shindychen.com/scribe.

Table of Contents

Introduction 1

The Handover 5

Part 1:
Beginnings 15

    First Touch 17

    First Make-Out Session 21

    First Blowjob 25

    First Love 29

    The First Time 33

Part 2:
Experiences 41

    First Time in a Car 47

    First Time on a Boat 53

    First Anal 57

    Second First Kiss 67

    London Town 71

    Epilogue 87

About the Author 97

Introduction

Greetings readers.

Thank you for spending your precious reading time with me.

I want to tell you about what's inside this book. It's for adults only.

The stories range from the innocent to the explicit, and are semi-autobiography, semi-fantasy.

If I help you become aroused while reading, more comfortable with your sexual self, or even enhance your sex life with your partner, then I'll consider it a huge compliment.

You're invited to join my author Facebook Page at facebook.com/shindychenwrites. I can't wait to hear from you! You can also contact me with stories of how this book has helped you by writing me at tft@thescri.be.

With Love,

Shindy Chen, Author

To my first Italian

The Handover

"Mr. Sidell will see you now."

Graham's icy assistant Theresa—the epitome of *sexy secretary* in her square-framed glasses, cream silk blouse, tight black pencil skirt, and sky-high heels—whisked me into his office at 11 a.m. sharp.

"He'll be right in," she said. *Was that a scowl on her face?*

"Thank y—," but the door closed before I finished. Not with a slam, but with authority.

Geez, who pissed in *her* cornflakes this morning. I took a seat in one of two Starck Ghost armchairs parked in front of a huge antique, dark-lacquered bureau.

Looking around, Graham's office was something out of Architectural Digest. My sister Marion was a budding interior designer and she'd cued me in on all her favorite furniture objets d'arts. I just never thought I'd have an opportunity to apply this knowledge—until now, and I suddenly felt a wave of gratitude for her efforts in culturalizing me.

There was a limited edition black-on-black leather and wood Eames chair in one corner. On the floor was a stunning antique red Samarkand rug, which featured delicate yellow and white flowers on its rectangular border. The same flowers were arranged again in diamond shapes as they converged toward the center. White peonies sat on the desk, next to a copper Moscow mule cup containing finely-sharpened black pencils, which oddly, were all pointed upward. In the middle was a single, limited edition white Mont Blanc pen mixed in for contrast.

Of course. This is also *exactly* how the office of the carefully-coiffed society man would look.

All I'd known of Graham was that he was one of New York's foremost magazine publishing editors—and that he was a dear friend of my late Aunt Elle. Or as most people knew her, the author Elle Weste; a girl-about-town turned journalist and bestselling author. She was a writer like me, only ten-times more successful.

When Elle was alive, she trusted Graham probably more than any of our family members. She mentioned "her best guy friend Graham" often, and I remembered seeing photos of the two of them at dinner parties and during nights out on the town—laughing and drinking with friends, all dressed to the nines.

After one tumultuous breakup Elle even spent a week on Graham's and his partner's couch until she set herself up in an apartment of her own. The story was that she hunted for her Upper East Side apartment, beat out the competition and signed the lease for it, *and* was all moved in by the end of the week—which in Manhattan is a pretty incredible feat.

Now, sitting in Graham's office, I smiled, bemused at how I even ended up here.

The weekend before, at a New York media titan's house party, my boyfriend Jack and I just happened to bump into Graham.

"Oh Graham, meet Olivia Weste—she's Elle Weste's niece," said one of Jack's colleagues. "Olivia, this is Graham Sidell."

"Umm yes, I know. I mean, yes, I'm Elle's niece."

I knew who he was immediately, and needed no introduction, but this *was* the first time I met the man in the flesh.

Graham did a double take, then peered into my eyes as if he was studying the contact sheets for one of his beautiful magazine spreads. He placed his hand on my shoulder and gave it a reassuring, fatherly grip.

"Pardon my staring, dear, but I've actually seen photos of you from when you were much, much younger! Elle was very proud of you girls. You have a sister, *younger* right? How are you two?"

"Yes, Marion is doing great—really great, thanks for asking." I was shocked he remembered any details about us.

"Wonderful. Well, Elle was a beautiful woman and a dear, dear friend. It's remarkable how much you look like her."

"Thanks." I guess? "We all miss her very much." I wasn't in the mood to talk about my dead aunt.

Sensing this, Graham added, "Well, what are you doing Monday? Come to my office; there's something I *must* give you—something that is yours to have. You won't believe it, but our meeting here tonight is quite serendipitous. You see, I always knew our paths would cross at the right time, and here the stars have aligned and made it happen."

He immediately pulled out his phone and skimmed his calendar.

"Yes, yes—I can see you between 11a.m. and just before I pop out for my lunch appointment."

Aside from all his "stars aligning" blather, all I heard was that Graham Sidell had something to give me—*me*? A lowly journalist with a *sometimes real estate, sometimes local* news beat? What could it possibly be?

"Umm, you have something to give *me*?" I asked.

"Something of your Aunt's that is actually yours to have. You know where the Hearst building is? Can you come Monday morning?"

"Wait, let me check." I opened my calendar. I knew my usual editor prep meeting ended at 10:30 a.m. but after that my schedule was clear until after lunch, so I could go from Flatiron to Midtown in time. Whatever Graham wanted, it had better be good; I wasn't in the habit of just traveling across town to meet with practical strangers.

"Okay, I can get there."

"Wonderful. Look, there's my assistant Theresa now. I'll have her book you in."

He slipped me his card, which I promptly took a picture of with my phone. I'm hopeless at keeping up with tiny pieces of paper, and stuffed his card and my phone back into my clutch. He gave me a quick kiss on the cheek and sauntered off toward Theresa.

What the fuck just happened? I was so wrapped up in our conversation that I didn't even realize Jack had moseyed off with his colleague. When he saw that Graham's exchange with me was over, he swooped in.

"What was that about? You look out of it," Jack said.

"He knew my Aunt." I said, dumbfounded. I looked across the room and saw Graham and Theresa looking my way, discussing me.

"Oh, wow, I'm sorry honey," Jack said.

Jack knew how close my aunt and I had been, and that she was my role model. He wrapped me up in his great big bear arms and I immediately felt better. "Let's go home. This party is starting to get lame," he said.

I looked around. Guys were huddled in one corner, sharing phone screens, talking, and laughing. The women were gathered in another corner, eyeballing the guys, and then the other women in the room, and then the guys, rinse, repeat.

Indeed, Jack always knew when it was time to bail. We left with Irish goodbyes, exiting quietly and quickly.

Graham sashayed in, breaking my reverie of last weekend's chance meeting. He took my hands in his, came in for a peck on the cheek, and seated himself behind the bureau.

He was fresh as a flower, wearing a navy Caraceni suit that hugged his body, and on his face sat round, horn-rimmed frames. If I wasn't madly in love with Jack, and if Graham wasn't gay, I'd be making bedroom eyes with this handsome silver fox.

Instead, he got right to it. "Your aunt was working on another book before she died. It was based on her journals."

Whoa. Hold the phone. Aunty never mentioned working on a book.

"Okay," I mumbled slowly, unable to say anything else.

He continued, oblivious to the equal parts anxiety mixed with confusion swirling in my body.

"And well, I have this manuscript; it's her memoir, of course, but I must warn you, it's a work of—how can I say this—erotica? It recaps her many first-time experiences and trysts with multiple lovers."

My mind was blown. Aunt Elle? My incredibly private, and discreet aunt who never brought anyone home, much less talked about her lovers, even when Mom pressed her like a lemon? My mother was, after all, a Southern housewife who lived for the juicy details of others' lives.

Aunt Elle's published works were always fictional, modeled only after the lives of dueling financiers and socialites, but never of her own.

"Well, how is it," I asked. "I assume you've read it."

"I have, but I can only place one or two of the stories based on whom she dated and when. The rest is more a chronicle of her first experiences with, *ahem*, many lovers."

"Wow," I said, trying not to sound like I'd been hit with a ton of bricks. I righted. "Well, why didn't you tell my Dad about this," I asked. "Or my grandmother?"

"Well, to be honest, I never knew how to approach your father or grandmother. What am I supposed to say, 'Hello, you don't know me, but your sister slash daughter wrote down all of her sexual exploits, would you like to read all about it?'"

"I guess not," I said. My cheeks flushed. I was annoyed at his mild sarcasm but also that any work of Elle's was held away from any of us, without reason, for so long.

"Don't be upset with me, dear. I said our meeting came at the right time, and here's why; the interesting thing about why I withheld this piece until now is this…"

Graham turned his gold MacBook Air around to my line of sight, and scrolled a few pages down.

There, in italicized font, read:

Dedicated to my dear niece, Olivia. Be free.

A shiver went through my body. I sucked my breath in slowly, like a slow-motion gasp.

"This is now yours to deal with however you wish."

"But—"

"No buts, dear. I know she would have wanted you, more than anyone else, to read it, and figure out what to do with it. With her gone and me finally meeting you, I'm now certain of it. I'll send over the digital file to you directly. Also, Theresa knows nothing about this, and I tell her everything. She's quite protective over me and she knew how much I loved your Aunt."

"I see." That explained Theresa's cold shoulder.

"Yeah, she's tough as nails with anyone she hasn't personally vetted for space in my calendar."

As if reminding himself of how valuable his time

was, Graham raised his eyebrows and pursed his lips, signaling the meeting was now over.

"Well, go on, dear. Don't make me regret meeting you and distrusting my impression that you could handle this."

"Okay, err, I mean, yes sir."

"Just call me Graham," he said with a warm smile. I imagine his charisma played a very big part in securing his present role.

After an awkward goodbye, and Theresa giving me a final once over, I walked out of the office, into a crowded elevator, and spilled out with everyone else into the bustling city street. I looked up at the building. Moments ago, from 30 stories above, these people were little dots, and the cars looked like Hot Wheels. I felt like I'd just emerged from some time warp.

I took a deep breath of the cold, brisk air. Could this really be my Aunty Elle's last work? I would be reading the words of a ghost.

When she died, I cried for days and even the sadness that came in waves was palpable. Hers was the first, and only funeral I'd ever attended; it was my first real confrontation with death.

I got my bearings. I was in Midtown Manhattan, at the corner of 58th Street and 8th Avenue, just a block from Central Park. The day was like any other for this part of the city, with tourists dodging taxi and car traffic, who were dodging Pedi cabs and even horse carriages. But for me, this was the strangest day I'd had in months, perhaps years.

I walked to the closest place I knew in the area, the Bottega Del Vino café on 59th Street and 5th Avenue, got seated in a comfy corner, and ordered a coffee and pain au chocolat. My phone pinged. I checked my inbox and there appeared a new email with the subject line, "Graham Sidell has made you a collaborator on the file TFT." I opened the email and saw a short message from Graham:

My dear, you now hold the key to your aunt's stories. Enjoy! ;)

I thought it a rather odd placement for a winking emoji, given I had no idea what he'd just offloaded. A link followed, labeled "TFT."

TFT? I clicked to accept. A tiny title appeared. I then pulled my iPad out of my navy-blue Longchamp Pliage, opened the file again, and there it was:

The First Time
A Collection of Firsts
By Elle Weste

Part 1:
Beginnings

First Touch

I can't remember the first time I actually came by touching myself. I imagine I must've been around 13 years old.

> *Who—Aunty Elle? I blushed. My head bowed over my iPad as if I was trying to hide an issue of Hustler magazine.*
>
> *But I checked myself; of course I was the only person who knew what I was reading—phew. None of the lunching ladies with their Birkins seemed to notice me at all, so I pulled my salmon-pink pashmina over my shoulders, and continued on. Now, where was I…?*

I can't remember the first time I actually came by touching myself. I imagine I must've been around 13 years old.

When I was younger, maybe 12, I remember

feeling something, a stirring every time my jeans rubbed up against my crotch a certain way. How it made my insides sort of twist, how my belly button almost tingled when I touched the little round bulb at the top of my vagina. I imagine that perhaps one day, I just kept touching and rubbing until I experienced a flush of sensation and liked it so much I kept at it.

But after I started doing it, I did this for a while, every afternoon after coming home from school.

It was my ritual; my parents weren't at home, so I'd lie down on the living room couch, watch some stupid afternoon talk-show, and then make myself come a couple of times or more.

Because I was young and had no idea what I was doing, this involved just rubbing myself over my underwear, until an exciting sensation built up, getting me so hot my ears burned and my heart raced.

I don't remember thinking about any boy or anything in particular. I just remember I liked the way this felt and I didn't feel guilty or ashamed about it afterward.

The easiest position for me to make this happen was on my stomach. So I'd lie there, and rub almost vigorously until I started climaxing, feeling the rush of endorphins, tension, and heat rising. This was the fastest route to an orgasm in under a minute or so. The feeling was just so quick and satisfying, and I'd often build one right after the other until I'd come two or three times, leaving myself breathless and exhausted.

I suppose all this practice in touching myself made it easier, and allowed me to understand my body—to be able to come while having sex with a partner or toy later in life.

First Make-Out Session

The first time I spent the night at my best friend Kirsten's house, I met Chris. Not only was he the first person I ever tongue-kissed, but he was also the first person I ever properly made out with. Talk about killing two birds with one stone.

Kirsten and I were both 15 and freshmen in high school. Her parents were away for the weekend. So, she and her sister—a cooler, older junior—decided to have a bunch of pals over for a party and sleepover.

Chris was also older. He was a sophomore at a different high school so we had never met each other before. In fact, there were about eight girls and guys there from other schools as well.

He was this heavy metal guy, wearing a black t-shirt and jeans; he wasn't the most attractive guy there but he had the whole dark, mysterious, sexy thing going for him.

I had no idea that Elle was ever into metal guys.

As the night went on, the others disappeared into their cliques and hideaways around the house and in the backyard, and began smoking joints and drinking beers.

Chris and I, eventually, found ourselves alone, just hanging out in the living room. He was stretched out on the couch with his head at on one end and feet at the other. I was sitting on the floor, in front of the couch, with my back leaned against the end where his head rested.

At the beginning of the night there had been no chemistry or attraction between us, but suddenly, an opportunity presented itself. We had the whole night to gradually explore the possibilities, without interruptions.

We got to talking and his hand drifted off the couch and onto my neck. He started caressing my neck and then my shoulders, and soon enough he bent his head down, and his lips met mine. His kisses were rough and hasty. When he stuffed his tongue in my mouth, the kissing became wet and sloppy.

After about 30 seconds of kissing, we came up for air. Out of the corner of my eye, I saw him wiping his mouth with the back of his hand but I wasn't going anywhere. I was determined to make this male specimen my sexual guinea pig. Up until now, I had been a total sexual novice and had never really made out with anyone.

So, we began again. I climbed on top of him on the couch. We started kissing again, this time with our bodies able to rub against each other. Through our clothes, I felt him getting rock hard in between my legs and pressing up against the inside of my thighs.

We continued making out and rubbing our bodies against each other until the wee morning hours. We were so exhausted we fell asleep—me on top of him.

When morning came, we woke up and gave each other a not-so-fresh kiss. I climbed off of him and with nowhere to go, went, as if dutifully, straight to the bathroom. Pretty romantic, right? I didn't think so either. When I pulled my jeans down, my crotch felt completely raw and bruised from all the dry humping, not that I really knew what that was—at least not yet.

As other partygoers woke up and entered the room, our guilty smirks pretty much gave away that we'd been up to something.

I only saw him once more at another house party. We looked at each other and then glanced away quickly, shyly, as if we as if we'd never even met. We were practically children, after all.

First Blowjob

The summer before my high school sophomore year, I attended a music camp in the artsy college town of Boone, North Carolina.

The guy I hooked up with wasn't even a camp attendee. He was a local boy named Connor whom I'd met from many nights hanging out at the only coffee shop in town, where people also met to mingle, and play trivia and board games.

Connor was Irish and had dark blonde curly hair and big pale-blue eyes. He was also super outgoing and charismatic. Once, as we played checkers at the coffee shop, he reached under the table and rubbed my knees and up my thighs. I thought he liked me. It wasn't until later that I learned he was just the village slut.

Another night, after we'd been hanging out all

afternoon, smoking pot, and bouncing around shops, we made our way back to campus.

I couldn't take him back to my dorm room; it wasn't a co-ed building. So we started making out on one of the university park benches. We soon realized we needed more privacy.

There was an embankment, with a huge underpass and lots of shrubbery and trees at both ends. We walked toward a dark corner of the underpass. I took my blue hoodie off, and he glared at me with a smirk on his face. I spread my hoodie down on the grass and sat on top of it, and he sat down close, right next to me. We were well hidden from passersby and we started making out again, with deep tongue kisses and heavy petting everywhere above our clothes, grabbing shoulders, each other's necks, and hips.

After several minutes, he stopped, unzipped his jeans, and whipped out his dick, which was large and hard. It was the first time I saw a dick standing on guard, straight up like that. In the faint moonlight, it looked like a big white spear.

"Kiss it," he said.

Without hesitation, I bent my head down and started giving the tip of his cock a few slurpy kisses. As he pushed my head down on top of it, I opened my mouth wider, unsure of what I was doing.

I eventually took the whole shaft in my mouth, working it deeper and deeper inside my mouth, until I felt the tip of his cock hit the back of my throat.

My mouth was opened wider than it had ever been before, to the point where I couldn't breathe.

He then guided my head up and down, up and down, on his dick, instructing me play by play.

"Suck a little harder...open your mouth wider... yeah, like that...oh, yeah."

In between his quiet groans and moans, a number of questions ran through my head: Is this what all the fuss is about? Can he feel my teeth? Am I doing this right? How long do I have to do this?

After what seemed like an eternity, I came up for air. My jaw was so sore, it felt like it was going to fall off. We began making out again for a bit.

He then stopped and spat in his right hand. He wrapped his hand around his dick, and began stroking it up and down as we resumed kissing. His breathing intensified. He stroked faster a couple more times and then jerked back and held his dick hard until he came. His come shot straight up into the air, landing on his hand and all over his boxers.

I just sat there, wide-eyed. It was my first time seeing a man come and it was fascinating.

We didn't have anything to wipe off with, so he grabbed my blue hoodie from out under me and wiped his hand off with it.

That fucking cum stain never did wash all the way out.

First Love

Andrew had long, naturally curly hair, and blue-grey eyes. He was also the first boy who made me feel special at the height of my teenage insecurity. Out of a sea of awkward high school guys, he was the only one I liked, and I was lucky that he liked me back.

We'd actually known of each other for a couple of years, first meeting in middle school. I thought he was cute and way out of my league, popularity-wise, because he was a year older than me. I never thought he'd eventually become my first love.

Things changed when I made it to high school. We found ourselves in a lunch calculus study group together—he told me he went every Tuesday—and though I hated calculus, I went back in hopes of seeing him there again.

Study group usually ended with about 15 minutes of free time before the last lunch bell rang. He would fill these precious minutes flirting with me and making me laugh with a mix of goofy, dorky, and intellectual jokes, and daily references to Star Trek or Star Wars.

Despite our different music tastes—punk music for me, and rock music for him—we found common ground in The Cure.

One day after the study group, there we were, with our mutual friend, Dave, when Andrew casually mentioned that he had a girlfriend. *Shit.*

She was a year older than him and attended a different high school, which made their situation seem even more exclusive and cool. This exalted him in my eyes, making him even more unattainable. But our flirtation continued, with him pointing out my funny handwriting, and me teasing him about his outfits, which usually consisted of ripped, frayed jeans, and Led Zeppelin or tie-dyed Grateful Dead t-shirts. I couldn't figure out if he actually liked me, or if I was just crushing on the wrong guy.

Soon, he started joining my clique during lunch. My high school was overcrowded, so kids were scattered everywhere during lunch, not just in the cafeteria, but also in the main assembly areas, outside walkways, and in the school's open lobby. This meant that he deliberately sought me out, because the lunch nook where I sat wasn't all that conspicuous.

The day that I'd been waiting for finally came. As lunch was ending, he announced that he and his girlfriend had broken up. He then asked me out.

On our first date, we went to see the movie "Alien." Not a typical date movie, but because we knew the guy working at the box office, we knew we could sneak in—it being Rated R and all.

At the end of our first date, he drove me home and we sat in his car at the end my driveway. There had been so much pent-up attraction between us for so long. The laughing, the flirting, the talking about our favorite bands and what instruments we played—which were the violin for me, and the electric guitar for him—and all the moments when it was *me* who I desperately wished he was referring to every time he mentioned anything about a girlfriend.

Rush started playing on the radio.

"I had a nice time," I said. "Thanks for taking me out."

"Yeah, that was interesting. I'm going to have to re-think the whole space travel thing. Those things just creeped me out."

"Yeah."

Our faces neared. My heart was racing.

And with that, he placed his super-soft lips on mine. We kissed for a solid five minutes but it was as if time stood still. Our lips moved slowly, as if in slow motion, and sweetly, and our tongues moved delicately together in each other's mouths.

It was innocent, sweet, and everything I thought our first kiss would be. I really liked this guy and nothing, not even my curfew, could take this moment away from us.

The First Time

After about six months of dating, Andrew and I decided we wanted to have sex. Not only were we each other's first loves, but we were each other's "firsts" as well.

The only problem was that Andrew didn't know he was *also* my first—I was a virgin but for some reason I thought my night making out with Chris counted at first as something more than making out. And just as silly young high school girls do, I exaggerated the details and once they stuck, I couldn't backtrack.

The enormity of lying about this didn't occur to me until later in life—I didn't know any better back then, I was young and stupid, and after the lie was told, it was too late to recant.

We planned on doing it at his place. His bedroom

was the entire space above his house's garage—"rec rooms" as they're still commonly called in suburbia.

Up until then, he had actually been more into doing it than I was. He wanted to get sex out of the way probably because he thought I was more experienced than him but, in truth was I was far less experienced than him.

The big night arrived.

His parents were out for the evening, and we were alone. It was quiet. We got naked and started making out. We had made out before, even been naked in bed together, but knowing what was about to happen left us both in a state of nervous excitement. In the moonlight, his tall, lanky body looked milky white against the dark covers. As he got on top of me, he had a look on his face of mixed fear and determination.

He placed his dick just on the edge of my lady parts, letting it rest there on my folds and lips, just for a second. Then, he made sure it was in position, and with one hard thrust he pushed straight inside me. As he entered, my eyes widened from a sharp sting, which was my womanhood being broken into by this foreign, hard phallus.

My cherry was popped.

"Does it hurt? Are you okay?" He asked, gently.

"No, keep going."

So he moved up and down, back and forth, slowly, and things started feeling slimy from my wetness. I don't remember particularly enjoying myself, rather than just being in a state of amazement and shock that I was actually losing my virginity. It was like I was having an out-of-body experience where my mind wasn't there, but my body certainly was a vessel to receive him.

He started moving faster and faster, with his dick going in and out, until he began climaxing. He withdrew, grabbed his dick with one hand, and came, making a low, grunting noise. Then, he fell on top of me. The whole thing was over in less than ten minutes.

Afterward, there was lots of kissing and cuddling on both our parts. It was an exciting intro to everything we'd only seen in movies and read about in books. We'd reached a new chapter in our relationship, and in our lives.

As we walked in his driveway toward my car, we could feel the cool air on our faces. Leaves were falling, some already draping the ground. I giggled.

"What?" He smiled, looking adorable.

"Nothing," I said, half teasing him but also not really sure what I was giggling about. Perhaps it was nervous laughter, perhaps it was out of relief for no longer being a virgin.

When I got home, I remember seeing blood mixed in with my post-sexual feminine wetness. Just a little bit, but not enough to count as a light period. I felt sore, but I wasn't in pain.

I climbed into bed, laid on my back, and smiled

to myself. Out of all the ways to lose your virginity, I'd say it was pretty high up there. The best.

"Miss, are you, eh, finished?" The waiter said, impatiently, in a thick Eastern European accent.

"Umm, yes, I'll have the check."

Startled, I looked at the time. 12:30 pm. I'd been sitting here, engrossed in Elle's words, for the past hour. It was no wonder I was being pushed out; they were eager to turn the table.

After the check arrived, I plopped down some cash and hurried back to work. I couldn't focus on work for the rest of the day; I was too wrapped up in Elle's words.

Later, I met Jack for dinner at American Cut, a steakhouse famous for its humongous tomahawk steaks. We didn't go to TriBeCa much. The scene was mostly bankers and their young families, but Jack had a late afternoon meeting in the area and was craving a steak.

When I arrived he was already at the bar waiting for me. The waitress whisked us over to the main dining room where we were sat in a corner booth.

Jack was in a good mood. He immediately started into a recap of his day.

"Oh my god, so today Joe and I were riding the F train up to Midtown, and caught these two old dudes fighting over a seat! He giggled, then shook from trying not to giggle, as he recalled it.

"Like, this old craggily white dude got all up in this old Asian dude's face, and was saying, 'I was sitting there, and you pushed me outta my seat.' And the Asian dude was like, 'You're a fucking idiot, this is my train, too!' And then the white dude was like, 'Just shut up,' and the Asian dude was like, 'You shut up!' And seriously these two old dudes were just going at each other for five whole minutes like two little five-year-olds. It was hilarious! Babe, you shoulda seen it. It was unreal!"

I just smiled at him with a blank stare.

"Hello-oooo?" He waved his hand in front of my face. "How was your day?"

"Very weird."

"Jeez, I couldn't tell," he said sarcastically. He smiled and put his arm around me. We settled back into the plush leather booth and I immediately felt at ease.

Jack and I had been dating for a year and a half, but after two months I knew he was different from all the other guys I'd dated before. Well not exactly "all the other," more like only one serious college boyfriend and a few randos after.

He had a youthful, "Andrew-McCarthy-from-

'Pretty in Pink'" look about him; a kind smirk in his resting state, which would turn to a dimpled, cunning smile when amused. One toothy grin and he could make any sour mood of mine disappear.

I told him about my meeting with Graham, about what Aunty Elle had written and left for me to discover, and how I read the first part of "The First Time" in one sitting. But most importantly, I recapped some details of her stories to him.

"Whoa, let me get this straight. Your aunt jotted down all her sexual schoolgirl fantasies and dedicated them to you?! Isn't that a bit weird?"

"Well, I think there's more than just schoolgirl fantasies there; they're actual experiences. And, I mean, I only read the first part. I haven't finished reading all of it yet."

"So turns out posh Aunt Elle was a total freak?"

"Stop it." There was no way I was going to allow anyone, least of all Jack, to smear Elle for me. "No one knows about it except for me. Well, and Graham, I guess. I mean, she left it for *me*. She dedicated it to *me*. Now I have even more of her memories. It's like discovering an entirely different side of her."

"You mean her sexual conquests. Wait a second. *I* wanna read it."

"No, absolutely not. At least not until I'm finished reading it first."

"Fine, be selfish. But in the meantime, if you come across anything juicy, *do* share. That would be *ex*-cellent," he said, steepling his hands and tapping them together à la Mr. Burns.

"No," I said, emphatically, but I also couldn't help grinning.

"Fine, suit yourself. So get all riled up from reading her booty stories and then come see me," he said with a raised eyebrow.

I rolled my eyes, blushing.

Our steak, fries, and salad arrived, and I went straight to stuffing myself, leaving the day and Elle's stories far behind.

Part 2:
Experiences

The Aunt Elle I knew was fabulous, beautiful, and whip-smart. She lit up the room wherever she went. She never made a scene. She was elegant, refined, and introverted.

In New York, Elle was a magazine writer. Her editorials graced the pages of Vanity Fair and Vogue. Her stark, black-and-white contributor headshots, featuring her dark mane, deep, almond-shaped black eyes, and pouty lips, often graced the front pages.

She always looked wind-swept in those stylized images, as if she'd been riding horseback along the Brazilian beaches of Trancoso.

She pretty much designed her own career to be exactly what she always saw herself doing. Regarding her personal life, she married only once, but then divorced just one year later.

"Everyone I know who is married, doesn't want

to be, and my girlfriends who've never been married, *desperately* want to be," she used to say. "And now that I've been there and done that, I'm fine just *being*. When did we start needing a milestone, a man or children to feel validated in any way?" At the time, I was too young to understand all this. But now, seeing my neurotic friends freaking out about having babies before they turned 30, I began to understand a little of what she meant. I was looking forward to having her guidance as I grew older and had relationships of my own.

But when I was about to start college at NYU, the news came suddenly and shockingly: at 45, Aunt Elle was dead.

That late summer evening, she was killed instantly by a drunk driver in a head-on collision on Malibu's Pacific Coast Highway. A restaurant patron had just finished partying at Nobu, stumbled into the driver's seat of her Porsche Cayenne, and drove right into oncoming traffic.

With Elle in the opposite lane, driving in a rented convertible roadster, she didn't stand a chance against the hulking SUV.

Given everyone's grief and shock after the accident, I volunteered to manage Elle's Facebook memorial page after her death. Though Aunty Elle hated Facebook, never interacting with it much while she was alive, she received outpourings of affection from it, messages that would leave me in an in-between state of happiness that she was loved, and overwhelming sadness that she was really gone.

Now, recounting Elle's life through her words was introducing this new side of her, the *memoir* side of her, and it was just downright surprising. It made me think about Elle's possessions. Her travel artifacts, souvenirs, and books were stowed away in boxes in my grandmother's house. Elle cherished her books most—not her designer clothes, shoes, jewelry, nor artifacts from around the world. I wondered if any other such journals remained from out of sight—whether untold stories such as these remained hidden. And with that, I resumed reading...

First Time in a Car

The first time I had sex in a car, it was with a much older guy; 25 to my 17.

His name was Gabe. We met the summer before my senior year of high school when I was at a camp for gifted students. Each student had an academic area of focus and mine was instrumental music.

By then, Andrew and I had broken up. Our sweet, young love had simply run its course.

The 8-week camp occupied a liberal arts college in a small town, so on our free nights some of us kids would break the boredom by finding amusing ways to entertain ourselves, smoking weed, and sneaking out into town.

One night, Kirsten came to town to attend a live show. And that's when I spotted Gabe. He was the drummer in one of three straight edge and metal bands who were performing that night.

Straight edge kids didn't drink or do drugs, and some even abstained from sex until marriage. Some announced to the world that they were straight edge by using Sharpies and magic markers to draw large X's on their hands. Some were also vegans.

Though I wasn't straight edge, we all became acquaintances through our respective friend groups. Our cliques meshed easily because we listened to similar music and dressed the same way. We mainly saw each other at live shows, where we met even more friends of friends.

After the show, Gabe wasn't too hard to find. He was one of the few African-American straightedge kids. Introductions were made, numbers were exchanged, and I learned he lived near my campus.

On our first date, he took me to a Thai restaurant—a vegan-friendly one that offered "mock" chicken and beef items on its menu. Over dinner, we discussed his lifestyle, and he told me how he thought I looked cute at the show in my Misfits ghost t-shirt. He also made it clear he was not one of the straight edge kids who abstained from sex. How lucky for me.

He was a gentleman, dropping me off back at camp promptly after our dinner. But on our second date, we went to his place, started fooling around and had sex for the first time. Gabe was also the first person who ever played with my ass during sex, tickling and penetrating it with his finger, to match the in-and-out rhythm as his dick stroked inside me, back and forth.

As camp came to a close, the future of our relationship was uncertain. I was leaving to go home and finish high school and we would be about an hour and a half away from each other by car.

I never called him my boyfriend, and it never occurred to me that we might continue our relationship beyond summer. We kept in touch, and he said he'd drive down to see me when he could.

One late August Saturday evening he came to my house while my parents weren't around.

Because my brother—

Wait a sec, I guess Elle meant MY father here. Weird. She hadn't mentioned anything about our family members until now. I kept reading.

Because my brother met him once and hated him ("*Elle, he's gotta be a loser. I mean, what 25-year-old needs to date a 17-year-old?*"), and also because I was weirded out about making out with him in my house, we drove around in my Jeep for a good 10 minutes just looking for a place to hang out.

We didn't want to spend too much time driving around either, because I only had a couple of hours before I had to get back, so we settled on a completely empty, and dimly lit, elementary school parking lot.

After we parked, we got into the back seat and started making out. I climbed on top of him, straddling him as he sat upright. He began unbuttoning my jeans, and we could both feel the heat rising between our bodies and inside the car.

I got back off him to kick my jeans off, and was naked from the waist down. We pulled his jeans and boxers down to his knees. I climbed back on top of him, returning to my straddling position. I could feel him getting hard underneath me, and I was getting wet with anticipation. I rose up, hovered over him for a second, we were tongue-kissing deeply, and then I lowered myself slowly and gently onto his dick. We both moaned simultaneously, feeling the pleasure overcome us and I took all of him deep inside me. Our bodies rocked back and forth, and as I went up and down with varying pressure each time my body swallowed him up, and my hips grinded against his, I stirred the deepest senses in my body as he filled me up.

He lifted up my shirt, undid my bra, and cupped both of my breasts in his hands. He placed his mouth over each breast, nibbling and sucking on my nipples. He grabbed my arms and held them to my sides, preventing me from moving as he lifted me up and down, slow, then fast, adding more power to each thrust of my body onto his dick, until our fucking became fast and the slapping, thudding sound of our bodies as they hit each other filled the quiet night.

As his thrusts became more rhythmic I knew he was about to come. When he came, he grunted, moaned, and shook violently. We ended up in a sweaty embrace as I felt the last pulses of his dick inside me.

As with most summer flings, the heat wore off. Eventually, by mid-autumn, I broke things off. I told him he was boring.

I was fascinated with the idea of being with someone so different than me, but even the whole straight edge veneer couldn't hide his total lack of personality. I had more pressing issues anyway, like finishing high school.

First Time on a Boat

I met Brian in a queue as we were waiting to take an overnight ferry from Portsmouth, England, to Caen, France.

This was when I was a university student in London, England, and I'd already traveled by train from London to Portsmouth. At the time, it was the most economical route to get from England to France, and the chunnel wasn't yet in full service.

I was going to France to meet my childhood French girlfriend at her university. They were throwing some sort of end-of-semester party.

Brian was American, from Chicago, and he was on his way to France's Normandy region to check out Omaha Beach. Apparently, his grandfather fought in World War II and the area was significant to him and his family.

He certainly had an all-American Ralph Lauren look. He was wearing a long, camel-colored overcoat, which covered dark trousers, a blazer, and a simple shirt. He had a cute, young Steve Guttenberg-like face, brown wavy hair, and said he was a young professional traveling overseas.

As it turned out, the ferry company felt bad that they had canceled my trip from the night before and so I was upgraded to a state room that had two bunk beds and a private bathroom.

He, on the other hand, was in the regular cabin, which included a long row of seating that resembled a movie theatre. This was merely a way to get from point A in England, to point B in France. It was not a cruise. The extent of the hospitality was onboard entertainment in the form of a lounge band, light bites, and of course, a bar.

We met for a drink. I felt bad that he would have to spend the whole night crossing the English Channel in practically nothing more than an armchair. So, after a few drinks and friendly, then flirty, banter, I boldly invited him to stay in my cabin.

When he arrived in my small state room, I assigned him the top bunk. We chatted bunk to bunk, then about half an hour later, he invited me up to the top bunk. I climbed up, fell on top of him and we started kissing and making out right away.

I pulled off my long-sleeved, powder-blue cotton pajama top.

"You have such a nice body," he whispered in my ear.

"Thanks," I said, coyly.

He wasn't so bad himself. He was of average build, skinny, with some muscles. We made out a bit more, and it became clear that we both wanted things to end only one way. Our movements felt closer and more passionate, our kisses firmer on each other's lips. We stripped off our clothes, piece by piece, until we were naked. I didn't object when he climbed off the bunk, rummaged around, and came back up with a condom. He put it on, and I didn't waste any time getting on top of him. I lowered my body and let him penetrate me slowly. As I began moving my body up and down, I realized I had to keep my body low, as I could barely ride him without my head hitting the low ceiling above. Despite the hot make out session, the sex was unremarkable and he came in less than 15 minutes. He went to the bathroom to clean up but by the time he returned I was already fast asleep.

When the ship docked, we emerged from my state room and he accompanied me to customs where we said goodbye. I saw my girlfriend waiting for me in the lounge. I walked toward her and saw him out of the corner of my eye hailing a taxi as we went our separate ways. We never exchanged contact details and I never saw Brian again.

First Anal

The first time I tried anal sex, I was 20-years-old.

It was with a Puerto Rican man named Layne, whom I met during my college spring break in Miami.

Anal sex! I could not believe what I just read. Jack kept putting the subject on the table, and here Elle was at 20-years-old already experiencing it! Or was I being a prude? After all, most of my friends had been vocal about their experiences, even how much they enjoyed it. I read on...

We hung out only once during spring break, but stayed in touch afterward through regular phone conversations. After about a month or so, I agreed to see him again, so he flew me down to Miami for a weekend.

When he picked me up from the airport, he was standing just outside of baggage claim, grinning ear-to-ear, and wearing a dark, flowing button-down shirt and dark grey trousers.

I stayed at his instead of booking a hotel.

In hindsight that may not have been the smartest or safest decision, after having spent so little face-time with him. But, our conversations made me feel like I knew him, and I felt safe in his presence—plus it was better than shelling out for a pricey hotel room.

Layne wasn't the typical, flamboyant Miami type. He wore glasses, sported a crew cut, mustache, and goatee, and was boyishly cute—and became handsome when he took off the glasses.

He was nerdy, not slick, and an avid comic and sports memorabilia collector and trader. This was his day job, and he would be on the phone with collectors and dealers from all around the world.

On the way back from the airport, as we were driving along the interstate, we hit a bump in the road and the hood of his brown Nissan Altima flew straight up in the air, almost hitting the windshield. "Whoa," he exclaimed, startled. I was too shocked to scream, unsure what this portended for the weekend.

He pulled over immediately, got out, and pushed the hood of the car down, just as another driver slowed down and asked if everything was okay. I didn't know whether to laugh or cry as I sat in the front passenger seat, watching the cars whizz by.

"Yes, we're good, thanks," Layne said, smiling, embarrassed, as he got back into the car. "Sorry about that!" He laughed. "Uh, welcome to Miami, baby."

For a second I considered bolting from the car but I gathered myself. *Don't be silly, it's fine.*

"It's okay, I just got a little freaked out," I said, even reassuring myself as the words came out of my mouth.

Layne lived in a nice one-bedroom apartment on the bayside. He treated me well that weekend. He took me to nice, but not over-the-top restaurants that were more popular for embracing the city's food and culture. One night, we even took his eight-year-old nephew out to a small sushi restaurant.

When we had sex, it was sweet. Not too rough or soft, but pleasant and attentive.

On my last day, we found ourselves lying in his bed, reading magazines. I was on my side next to him, with my head resting half on his shoulder, half in his armpit nook.

We were cuddling, kissing, and making out in between reading tidbits from articles out loud to each other.

He moved so I fell more on his body, less on his arm, and his hand pressed firmly on my back. He lowered his head and kissed me deeply, as he slid his hand down until it was firmly on my ass.

I felt his fingers creep their way under my shorts, finding my underwear, and then caressing my pussy. He'd rubbed gently only a few times back and forth before I could feel my wetness surging, and my pussy throbbing.

We started having sex. As I was on top of him, riding him back and forth, I felt his right hand grabbing the top of my thigh. Then he shifted his hands underneath me and I felt his fingers beginning to play with my ass. His fingertips were touching, pressing, and inserting just inside the rim. I shifted my body onto one finger so that it went deeper. I wanted to feel more of it inside me.

This was a new, tingling sensation and my body welcomed it. Gabe had only played with my ass, but we never took it further to actually having ass sex.

He spanked my butt with his free hand, and then he used both arms to flip me over so I laid flat on my stomach, my legs spread out before him as he sat in between, on his knees.

He started rubbing my pussy with his thumb, slowly and softly, making me wetter. I was so horny from the teasing and the torture, that my hips moved in a way that begged to be pounded into and filled up again.

He then reached over to his nightstand, rummaged around for a bit, and squeezed a bit of lube on his finger, which he then rubbed on the rim and inside of my ass, and on his dick. I knew what he was thinking and I didn't fight it, I was nervous and excited.

He moved his body so that it hovered over me and placed his dick right on top of my ass, letting it sit there for a moment, as I took in this new sensation. He slowly slid his dick in, and I sucked in my breath at the initial pain. The sensory experience was unlike when I lost my virginity, this pain was more acute. He nuzzled his face into my neck and hair, and I was comforted immediately.

"Do you want me to keep going?"

"Yes."

I let my body go and relaxed. As he slid his dick inside my ass more, I was reminded of how big his cock was. It felt soft upon entry, but once inside me, he was rock solid.

The more relaxed I was, the more turned on I became. When he was mostly inside me, he moved slowly in and out; we were both on our sides as if we were spooning, and the angle suited me better, allowing me to enjoy what was happening rather than feeling any pain.

With his left hand, he reached around and stroked my clitoris as he was giving my ass slow, deep strokes. He kept giving my neck soft kisses, which drove me even crazier.

We shifted so that my body resembled a yoga child's pose, but my knees were wider apart. He began thrusting harder and I understood he wanted to come. I welcomed the dull, aching pain that came with each thrust. Finally, I felt his body seize up and his groans became deeper. He let out one last deep grunt and a small cry as he penetrated me one last time, coming deep inside my ass.

Afterward, we showered together and I felt giddy, as if I'd experienced losing my virginity all over again. I was happy that he took it slow and took it easy on my body. Surely I'd never expected him, nerdy Layne, to be this sexual adventurer. But that made him even more appealing, even perhaps made me want to see him again.

After I flew back, we talked only a few more times by phone, lost touch, and never saw each other again.

It was Sunday night, and Jack and I were in the middle of what had become our ritual, which consisted of us lounging in his queen-sized bed. He was sprawled out next to me, and our bodies were wrapped up in his luxurious grey 600-thread-count Egyptian cotton sheets. The man was meticulous about his sheets.

The weekend had gone by quickly and I'd been engrossed in Elle's words for most of it.

Every free moment I had, I'd picked up my iPad to read from where I left off.

One thing was clear; I was a lot less experienced

than Elle at her age, and perhaps even now at 25-years-old.

For instance, Jack had hinted at us trying anal sex after only 6 months of dating, but he was always quickly rebuffed. After that, it seemed he brought it up every moon phase. The last time he nudged was during our two-year anniversary trip, when we drove upstate to the Bedford Post Inn.

When we were making love in a position where I was on my fours and he was behind me, he pressed his finger on the rim of my ass and that aroused me, but when he placed his dick on it, I quickly moved away, letting out a muted, nervous shriek. He didn't say anything, he just turned me around as if in defeat and we finished making love with him on top.

Some of my girlfriends happily divulged that they'd tried it and liked it, no, rather, *loved* it. Even one of my more expressive girlfriends said that she was happy to experiment with her husband in the bedroom. She figured that if he had any sexual fantasies to fulfill, she would be the one to satisfy them rather than him getting it anywhere else.

My thoughts came back to Jack's bedroom. Lately we'd been spending nights at his place. He would never admit to it, but he preferred staying at his because it *was* nicer than my place, which was a small one-bedroom on the first floor of a classic, five-floor walkup building in Yorkville on the Upper East Side.

Jack's apartment on the other hand was in one

of the many new, glass shard-like buildings piercing the sky in gentrified Hudson Yards, which was in the artsy north Chelsea district of Manhattan.

He certainly worked hard and moved up quickly in his career, but he'd also been given a leg-up from his many connections cemented by his family's wealth, schooling, and university network. In New York this could improve one's life significantly, even down to the apartment hunt. When Jack was apartment-hunting, he placed a call to a friend whose family was developing the condo where he now lived. Within mere weeks he was in with no competition, no sweat. In fact I don't even think he paid the standard security deposit requirement of first and last month's rent.

I looked at him. He was shirtless, and had his matte-black Warby Parkers resting at the end of his nose. He was deeply engrossed in the latest Wilbur Smith adventure on his Kindle. He looked so adorable and handsome to me in these moments— as a calm, relaxed, bookworm, even better than when we were out at late-night parties, galas, and dinners. It turned me on. Lucky for me that I had a masterpiece of a man at my side.

He didn't notice that I was checking him out. I leaned over and caught some words on his Kindle. All I could make out were the words "incandescent" and "plundering," likely describing some sort of bedroom heroine-takedown scene.

"Hey! Stop spying."

"Ha! You were so into it! No wonder you didn't notice that I've been checking you out for the last five minutes."

"You sure it was only five?" He chuckled. "Because I'm frickin' HOT!"

I rolled my eyes but couldn't help smiling.

"I mean, of course you were checking me out, especially if you were reading the 'I'm a closet freak' book," he said with exaggerated winks.

"Oh, shut up, Jack." I let out a sigh of disgust, and turned to the opposite side of the bed, closing and placing my iPad on the night table.

"Hey come on, don't get mad! I'm *just* joking."

Again, with the jokes.

"I mean, I guess I'm just a little surprised that the aunt you looked up to all these years has a complete naughty side. So anyway, what did you just read about?" I felt him rise up on his elbows, talking to my back.

"Anal sex," I blurted out matter-of-factly, staring at the night table lamp.

"Whoa-ho!" He paused. Then, as he walked two fingers onto my hip, he asked gently, "So, does that mean you're ready to try it?" He was trying to be super nice, and I could tell he was asking with a smile, and likely wide eyes, too.

"No, not ready."

I felt his body almost deflate as it slumped back into the bed.

"I'll let you know when I'm ready," I said.

"Okay, babe. I'll be waiting with bated breath." I sensed a tinge of annoyance in his voice. He pulled himself close and planted a big wet kiss on the back of my neck.

"Are you done reading," I asked.

"Yeah, I'm done. It's late." He laid on his back and stretched his arms above his head.

I kept my back turned toward the night table. Would I ever be as free or open with my sexuality as Aunt Elle? Why were some women so experimental and free and so confident and why was I so unwilling? I loved Jack more than anything and I trusted him more than any guy I'd been with before. Why was I afraid to explore sexually with him? I wondered if I'd ever get "there."

"Lil—. Hey Lill…" I could hear Jack whispering in my ear, in a soft soothing tone.

Those were the last words I heard before I drifted into a deep sleep.

Second First Kiss

The first time I kissed a woman I was 34-years-old. I thought this was fairly late considering my collective sexual exploits up until then.

I'd always been curious about what it was like and when it would happen. After all, I had never been in an amorous relationship with a woman, yet always appreciated the beauty of the female form. I'd even found myself attracted to certain women over the years, yet had never pursued any of them intimately.

It happened at a gentleman's club on Manhattan's West Side. I was there with four other friends, two guys and two girls.

We booked a private room and started our own party, inviting four beautiful dancers in with us. There was a blonde girl, a tall Caribbean girl, and two Latina women. My girlfriend spoke to the dancers in Spanish, and found out one was Dominican and the other Colombian.

Even in the champagne room, these girls were just teasing our guy friends, power seductresses they were, shimmying and grinding their booties, sitting on them, straddling them, grinding as they danced, letting us spank their booties as they twerked.

But when giving lap dances for girls, dancers are more comfortable skirting the rules. They're a little freer, nastier, They let girls get closer, they let them touch.

After half an hour into our party, bottles were popped, drinks were flowing and the music was loud. Everyone was dancing and having a good time. It was our very own club in a space smaller than the size of a New York studio apartment.

After giving the guys several lap dances at the girls' requests, the men in the room told the dancers to swap and the Colombian girl started dancing for me. She had her back toward me, and I saw her pale, creamy, tight ass shaking with the music. She lowered and sat her body onto mine, putting her head on my chest, slowly moving her body up and down to the music.

When she stood up and turned around, she hovered over me and her hands grazed and caressed my arms, while her hips were slowly moving from side to side in front of my face. She smelled like a mixture of citrus, florals, and candy, like the overpowering scent that hits your nostrils when you walk by a Bath & Body Works store, only in this case I couldn't make my escape. She let her hands drop down to caress my legs, sliding them up my skirt, up and down several times, each time stopping innocently short of my crotch. Had she gone further she would have realized I wasn't wearing any underwear.

She leaned her body into me, and her face came closer to mine. Her long, brown wavy hair cascaded down over my head, concealing both of our faces and serving as a shade to block out everyone else in the room.

Slowly, her lips stopped short of mine, and I moved my face up so that my lips met hers in a gentle kiss. Her lips were softer than any man's lips I'd ever kissed. We weren't kissing hard, rather gently, and I felt the tip of her tongue graze my lips. I stretched my tongue out to meet hers, just above her lips. In that short, intimate moment, I felt the heat of arousal surge through my body, which dissipated when we stopped kissing and she finished dancing. The song changed. After that, she spent the rest of the evening dancing for all of us, but I left knowing I wanted to try it again.

I scrolled further...there weren't any other full chapters. I held my tablet close to my chest, closed my eyes, and took a deep breath. I just finished Elle's last words to me, or at least what Graham had sent to me.

This—what did it all mean, her dedicating this sexual journal, or whatever it was, to me? What was the point of it all? Elle had certainly influenced my writing, even encouraged me to begin journaling as early as age 13. A best-in-class high school essay, followed by an editorial column and university newspaper articles, convinced me that I might actually possess a little talent to cultivate.

Perhaps this was her way of encouraging me to fulfill my desires—sexual or not. During our family vacations she was always the one daring me to try new activities, to overcome my fear and learn how to surf, sail or scuba, to ride our bikes and explore new territory.

I was a little offended that Elle thought I might not be as ballsy as she was, and that she felt a guide might be necessary to help show me the way. I certainly wasn't, nor did I want to be a mini-Elle. But I know she meant well and just wanted me to find my spirit all along.

London Town

Jack and I were in London. He was there for work, and I'd tagged along. As expected, since we arrived he had been running around like a chicken with its head cut off, so I was left to wander the city streets on my own, which suited me just fine.

I relished the thought of exploring by myself, but really just needed a respite from work. It had been super-crazy lately with too many multiple, last-minute deadlines piled on *and* of course I wanted some time on my own to think about Aunt Elle's journal and what, if anything, I would do about it.

When would I go back to Graham? What would I say to him? Or should I just keep the file locked away from everyone and keep it *my* secret? I wanted a full, free day to think.

When in London, I always felt the need to have a traditional high tea; the event was one of few quirky Britishisms that just made sense to me.

On this particular day, I chose the Langham Hotel for my high tea and the ambiance was everything I wanted; quiet, serene, and elegant. Nothing was more soothing than a cure-all cup of hot tea, accompanied by warm sultana scones smothered with thick clotted cream. Of course, no high tea would be complete without a bevy of savory and sweet treats like salmon toast, cucumber sandwiches, macarons, fruit tarts, and chocolate truffles.

After tea, I bounced down to Selfridges on Bond Street. After poking around in the shoe gallery on the 5th floor, I made it down to the ground level Food Hall. This was no ordinary food hall; there was every possible snack or meal imaginable, along with a gourmet grocery store. But I was there for a very American export...Krispy Kreme.

I lined up to buy a couple of glazed donuts so that Jack and I would have some sweet treats later. Because this was more like a food counter and not a standalone shop, there was no "hot and fresh" red neon light. The donuts weren't coming off the conveyor belt, but these would just have to do.

After Selfridges, I visited Top Shop just nearby. I was poking around the denim section when I sensed someone's eyes on me. I looked up and saw a woman with dirty blonde, bedhead hair staring at me from a few racks away. She was wearing an oversized blazer over a white t-shirt and black skinny leather trousers. From what I could make out, she had a delicate, pretty English face and rosy lips.

She looked down immediately as I caught her eyes.

I shrugged. She must've been checking out my outfit. That morning I made a point to dress more "London-y" opting for a long dark floral dress, topped with a leather motorcycle jacket.

After 10 minutes of perusing some high-waisted jeans, I grabbed two pairs to try on, and sauntered over to the fitting room. I expected a massive wait but was pleasantly surprised to find it completely clear. Perfect timing.

"You can go to the third room on the right, yeah," said the store associate.

I made my way down the hallway, and noticed the curtain gaping halfway open to the second stall.

As I walked by it, I quickly glanced inside and saw the same blonde woman from before, but now she was topless. In fact she was naked except for a lacy black thong.

I paused. Her cute, perky tits and pale-pink nipples were out and visible from a side profile. While I knew I should look away, I was drawn by this free peep show. My eyes remained fixed open.

She was hanging up a dress when suddenly, she looked into a corner of the mirror's reflection and saw me there, staring at her.

Shit! I turned away immediately, and rushed into my stall. *Did she think I was checking her out?* I mean,

I kinda was, but more out of fascination, less out of sexual interest. I didn't dare peek or look out into the hallway for fear of seeing her again.

Inside, I held my breath and stood so still as to not make a peep. I looked in the mirror. I was embarrassed at my slight voyeurism and my face was flushed. I gathered myself.

Every time I traveled to a foreign city, if I was in a taxi and looking at, or just walking by houses, I'd peek inside people's homes—at the artwork, furniture, colored wallpaper, plants—for any glimpse into how the residents of that particular city lived.

Jack called it nosiness. But I'd looked at this woman's body in the same way as I did when I'd strain to look into these people's ways of living, and I was also a little envious that I didn't have such a hot skinny body, or cute tits like hers. My nipples were dark, and my circular areolas were dark and large, too.

I shook my head and put my bag down, almost forgetting where I was. I recalibrated and got undressed, and slid the first pair of jeans on. Hmph. This tiny fitting room didn't provide sufficient scale for me to properly assess how my butt looked in them. I would have to emerge from the fitting room and walk to check myself out in the full-length mirror at the end of the hall. I peeked my head out of the fitting room and looked left.

Her stall was now empty. Phew.

"New jeans?" Jack said, checking my ass out as we were making our way to our seats.

"Why yes. I bought them today. I'm surprised you noticed!"

"They look nice. They give your bum a nice little lift."

"Bum?" I teased.

"Hey, we're in London, aren't we? 'When in Rome,' as they say. It's your *bum*, not butt, *innit,*" he smirked.

That cockney slang. One of Jack's best friends was from North London, and taught him all sorts of useless British-isms that Jack often liked to sprinkle in his conversation, but with 10 times the frequency now that we were actually in London.

Jack came straight from a work meeting to meet me for dinner at Chiltern Firehouse. We were now out for after-dinner drinks on the rooftop of a member's club in East London. I was sipping on a vodka mule, and Jack a reposado on the rocks.

As usual it was brisk in the evening, so the hip fashion-y and art-y cliques were in their jackets and tailored blazers, all huddled under heat lamps stationed around the pool.

Jack's French friends, Arnaud and Christian, were also with us and we all four began a lively conversation to catch up on work, living in London versus

New York, and what great new restaurants to try in our respective cities.

By our third round of drinks, which became vodka sodas for all, Arnaud was quite inebriated. His French accent noticeably thicker, his movements expressive, and his body language more animated than before.

The more drinks Arnaud had, the more hands-y he became with everyone around him, touching on the arm, touching on the leg, putting his arms around you, no matter guy or girl. He could get away with it because he always so charming, handsome, and superbly dressed. He certainly had a naughty side which I'd mentioned to Jack before but he always brushed it off. In other words, if you wanted to do or try anything crazy, perhaps even criminal, drunk Arnaud was the perfect wingman.

I began people-watching as the guys engaged in a lively debate over French politics.

"But non! You cannot have it two ways. Zere is simply no solu-shon. People want her to be just like her father, but she is less conservative than him."

"Well sure you can, you simply copy what's worked before..."

I had no idea what they were arguing about, something about Le Pen and the upcoming French election but I generally avoided political discussion when out, and especially when alcohol was already in the mix.

Suddenly, a woman's voice interrupted.

"Hey Stranger."

Arnaud looked up.

"Sophie! Oh, mon dieu!" Arnaud leapt up immediately, and proceeded to faire la bise with this blond woman who'd crept up on the edge of our circle.

"Mais, que fais-tu à Londres? Tu me manques!" Arnaud exclaimed. "Everyone, zees ees my dear friend Sophie! Eh, we sat together for my whole year of business school! Assis-toi!"

"My friends and I were just leaving, and then I saw you sitting here and had to come say hi! I would recognize that face anywhere," Sophie exclaimed, in a British accent.

"Woo hoo! Of course, you must stay! Join us, we need to catch up," exclaimed Arnaud.

"Mais bien sur. I'm not ready to turn in yet, but they are," she said, giving him a tiny wink while gesturing toward her friends at the other end of the rooftop by the exit. "I'll be right back, let me tell them I'm hanging around here."

Sophie walked back to her group, and kissed them goodnight. When she walked back she was graceful, like drifting through air.

"Ah, you've returned. Have a seat, *please*!" Christian said, shuffling to make space next to him. Of course, he was always on the lookout for fresh meat. She sat down next to him, and directly opposite me.

Our eyes met.

Oh, mon dieu indeed.

It was *her*. Top Shop fitting room girl. And here, on the rooftop, under the lights in the night sky, she looked absolutely stunning. Her blonde hair was twisted in a low chignon. Her cheekbones were taut, her rosy lips even rosier than I remembered, with a hint of gloss. Her eyes were crystal blue.

"Hi, I'm Olivia," I said, extending my hand out, and smiling.

"Hello, I'm Sophie." She smiled warmly and took my hand in hers, giving it a gentle squeeze and then shaking it slightly, with a loose, informal grip.

It was strange. I felt nervous, like a little girl who was speaking to her crush. I began blushing. *Oh my god, oh my god, oh my god. Did she recognize me from the fitting room?*

Turns out Arnaud and Sophie hadn't seen each other in a couple of years. They proceeded to catch up for about 15 minutes, as the boys listened in like flies on the wall, interjecting with questions when they could.

After business school Sophie moved to Paris, and Arnaud stayed in London. Only recently had she returned to London to work on expanding her business as a full-time personal stylist.

Another round of drinks arrived, but this time I only drank from my bottled water. I was feeling a little woozy. I began thinking...instead of resolving what to do with Aunt Elle's manuscript, I spent the whole day shopping and wandering about London.

I'm sure Graham was curious whether I'd read it all. I hadn't emailed him since he handed it over.

I pulled out my phone and started drafting an email:

> *Graham, I've finished Elle's manuscript now. Let's meet one day next week if you're available.*

I hit *SEND*.

I'd pick his brain on next steps. Graham would know what to do. Phew, done. Now I felt like I'd been a little bit productive today.

I looked up. The boys were clearly loosened up from their drinks, excited to have a new female in the mix. They picked up their raucous, giddy conversation from before, their laughing even more amplified.

Sophie and Arnaud had finished waxing poetic about how they came to be where they were now.

She turned to me. "So, do you live in London?"

I had just taken a full swig of water and almost choked, trying to speak.

"Oh me? Umm, ahem, no, Jack and I live in New York," I said, wiping the side of my mouth.

"How lovely. I *love* New York—I visit often—the shopping, the energy, the restaurants...and there's always a new place to eat."

"Oh yes," I exclaimed. Okay, so far so good. It didn't seem like she recognized me at all. *Stop being awkward, stop being awkward.*

"So, how long are you in town?"

"Oh? Us? We're only here two days. We leave the day after tomorrow."

"So then do you also live together, in New York?"

"Oh, no, not yet. I mean—no. We might soon, as soon as my lease runs up." I realized I was rambling a bit, and nervous.

"What about you? I mean, where do you live in London?"

"Oh, well, I'm waiting for my flat to be finished right now, and a few furniture and artwork deliveries. My flat's just near here. It's just been painted today, actually, so I'm staying here in the hotel for now, but just for a couple of days."

"So you're staying *here*? How are the rooms? I've only seen them online. I've never stayed here."

"Yeah, it's really nice," she said. "Cozy," she said with a laugh. "Charming."

"Mmmmm hmmm," I nodded, sounding interested, but just trying not to be weird.

"Alright ladies, let's wrap this up," said Jack of all sudden. "Sorry babe, but I've got an early morning."

"Oh no, but we were just getting started," Sophie cooed.

"Ha, and are you out for the rest of the evening," Jack asked.

"No, not at all. I was just joking. I've had meetings and been out all day so I'm ready to head to my room."

"Oh my, well then you ought to get to bed," Jack said, with a smirk, flashing his million-dollar smile.

Was he flirting with her?

"Wait, where do you stay in London," he asked.

"Well, I was just telling Olivia I'm staying here for a few days until my flat's ready. It's being refurbished, you see. And, actually, Olivia was curious what the rooms here look like."

At this point I was more studying Jack's flirty face, and less listening into their conversation. I was also beginning to feel tired as well from my day out, dinner, and now the drinks.

As they talked, he was smiling and Sophie was doing the whole coquettish flirty-girl thing. What the fuck. If I wasn't here, he could easily have gotten her number.

Jack rose to say goodbye, giving Arnaud and Christian bro hugs. "See you dudes, maybe tomorrow," I overheard him saying.

Jack looked at me. "Shall we go, babe?"

"Are you guys really leaving," Sophie asked me and Jack. "I mean, do you want to smoke a bit?" She smiled secretively, and raised one eyebrow. Hmmm. The thought of a little weed to mellow me out *did* sound good.

"And Olivia, you could then check out the rooms here? I have one of the nicer ones, at least I think," she said, jokingly.

"Umm..." I looked at Jack, eyes wide, not sure what to say.

"Oh, he doesn't care. Do you Jack?" She looked at him, and I think she even batted a lash.

Jack shrugged with crossed arms. "Sure, why not!? You twisted my arm."

"Great, come on."

Sophie announced to the group she was retiring as well, and said goodbyes to Arnaud and Christian, promising she'd be in touch with Arnaud soon. They kissed each other goodbye and hugged. She grabbed my arm and I grabbed Jack, and we all made our way to the lift.

We heard Arnaud yell out, "Bye now! Don't get yourselves into too much trouble! Much love, à bientôt my brother!" I glanced back and waved. The two looked a little deflated that their night was drawing to a close.

When the lift reached her floor, she led the way out and straight to her room. I noticed she had the same skinny leather trousers on from earlier that afternoon.

She whipped out her key swiftly, as if she'd had it on the ready all night, and opened the door to a room with a nice big bed. It looked so comfy and tempting, all I could do was surrender and wander toward it, plopping down with hopefully a little bit of grace.

Jack helped himself to an armchair in the corner of the room, letting out a big sigh as he sat down, just like he did when he got home after a long day at work.

Sophie hit a few buttons on her phone and on came upbeat EDM-type dance music. She punched a few buttons into the room safe and fished out a pre-rolled joint. She lit it, and took a long drag.

I felt a little dizzy and the room was starting to spin. *Damn alcohol!*

Sophie walked over and sat down next to me on the edge of the bed.

"Are you okay?" She asked with a smile and a gentle shoulder nudge toward me. "This will make you feel better."

"Sure, I think I drank too quickly, or maybe didn't sleep well last night from the jetlag."

She passed me the joint, and I noticed the word LIT in block letters printed in patterns all along the joint paper.

"This is cute," I said, taking a couple of hits. She was right, I immediately felt better and calmer.

"Oh, I got those papers in this bodega in L.A. Cute, right?" I nodded, blowing out smoke from my exhale. "I don't know, I'm more of a traditionalist rather than using the new vapes."

I passed the joint to Jack, who took a couple of long drags. He the rose up out of his chair to check out the view from the window.

"Nice," Jack said. "Hey, Sophie, do you mind if I just use the bathroom?" With a smirk and mock

British accent, he corrected himself and said, "Oh, pardon meh, I meant the *loo?*"

"Oh sure, hon, it's right over there."

Sophie gestured toward the bathroom door. Jack went, leaving me and Sophie alone.

She moved closer, toward me. I could see her lip stain still looked fresh and that her cat eyes were drawn with a fine dark brown eyeliner. She was so close I also caught a whiff of her perfume for the evening. It was some sort of smoky, amber essence.

The music was just loud enough to drown out Jack bumping around the bathroom.

"I remember now, it was you. I thought you looked familiar."

"What? What do you mean?" *Oh my god. Oh my god.*

"Earlier today, it was *you* at Top Shop. I saw you. And you saw *me.*"

My heart began pounding. I could feel my face beginning to get hot and flushed.

"Oh my god, I'm so embarrassed," I blurted out. "I mean, I was just walking by, and then tonight I knew you looked familiar when you sat down!" *Stop sounding like an idiot.*

"Don't worry about it. You're fine." She grabbed my hand. "In fact, you're gorgeous."

She held my hand tighter and our eyes met. She was sexy. I could feel heat stirring in my hips and between my legs.

I squeezed her hand back, and she guided it toward her, placing it on her waist first, and then moving it upward so it rubbed against, and landed firmly on her breast. I could feel her nipples—the pale pink nipples—small and taut, through her silk blouse.

"I know you liked what you saw."

I was speechless. I tried to form a word, but I couldn't. I was mostly just mesmerized. I'm sure I was beet red, beyond blushing. What was happening? I was a mix of intoxicated, tired, and now a bit high, which meant I was also a little horny.

She made her next move and came in for a kiss, slowly. As she planted her lips on mine, my eyes widened. The sexual energy in my body surged. I wanted this. I wanted her. Her lips were soft, with a hint of vodka. When her tongue crept in between my lips, I also tasted the peppermint gum in her mouth. I kissed back, leaning my head in.

This was a first for me. I mean, I'd kissed my best friend once during a truth or dare game when we were 14, but it was only a quick peck—it was nothing like this.

Sophie moved her hands up to the back of my head and pushed me closer in. We kissed harder, firmer. I could feel her sucking the air out of my body and our tongues were now playing with each other, deeper inside each other's mouths.

Oh my god. Jack. I wondered if he was wondering why we were so quiet. I breathed in.

She must have sensed my sudden paranoia. "Shhhh. Don't worry. He won't mind," she said, eyes closed.

"But—"

"One second." She got up, and walked over to the door. She picked up the hanging *Do Not Disturb* placard, opened the door, and placed it on the front, and then gently closed the door. She looked back at me, with smiling eyes and a small grin as if we'd just shared an intimate joke.

Jack emerged from the bathroom, and seeing her at the door, smiled a polite smile and asked, "Oh, are you going somewhere?"

"No," she replied. "I'm fine, and we're all staying right here." She smiled back at him, and then me.

She took his hand and led him toward me, so it was just the three of us in the center of the room.

Epilogue

October 15, 2016

When she got up to put the lock and DND sign on the door, Jack came out of the bathroom. She turned down the lights, grabbed Jack's hand and led him to the bed and they started kissing.

You'd think I would've been upset by it, but I actually didn't mind at all. When he saw that I was smiling and didn't object, he continued kissing her.

She began unbuttoning his shirt, took it off, and then started undressing herself. We ended up the three of us in bed with Jack between us on opposite sides. I undid his pants and pushed them down his legs, and undressed myself. We were all naked, rubbing, feeling each other skin, familiar and new with no concept of time.

Jack began kissing me, and she was nuzzling her face behind his ear and the back of his neck, with her arm draped over him, caressing his chest down to his thigh. I stroked his dick. I rubbed and grabbed on his balls with my free hand. I could hear him softly grunting from the sensory overload.

We continued like this, kissing and touching until Jack rose himself up on his elbows, and moved from being in the middle. I took this moment to find Sophie's lips and I rolled my body over on top of hers, grinding my hips into her crotch. She looked like she was in complete bliss, and I was happy to see her face contorting in ecstasy. *I was the one making her feel good.*

Jack was now behind me and I felt his arms lift my waist up in the air, so that I was on my fours with the front of my body propped up on my elbows, and Sophie was underneath me. I continued kissing her deeply. I shrieked as Jack penetrated me from behind, practically impaling me with his first thrust, followed by slow, deep strokes in and out, his hands alternating, grabbing between my hips and asscheeks, moving me back and forth.

He reached around my thigh and started rubbing me on my clitoris slowly, just above where his dick was inside me. He stroked his fingers up and down, playing with me by alternating between rubbing my clit and tapping it softly, working me up, while his dick kept filling me up, back-and-forth. At one point I even put my hands on his to slow his fingers down, as my whole clitoral area was becoming super-sensitive to his touch. I felt my wetness all over his hands.

Sophie saw us, and she reached down to touch herself as she watched Jack fucking and touching me. In this height of pleasure—being pounded from behind and having my clit stroked, while watching her face react to her touching herself—I was overwhelmed in my own state of euphoria, feeling the beginnings of an orgasm building from deep within. After all the years of acrobatics-style and doggy-style sex, I'd never come on my fours, and I wasn't going to fight it.

My body began responding to the rhythm. I moaned softly every time he filled me up. I also felt her body begin to tense and flow with mine as she continued rubbing herself—slowly, quickly, slowly—to match our sexual rhythm.

I began to climax and I wasn't going to let it go. I let it build and build until it seized my entire body. Jack kept at his strokes and I craned my neck up as I held tightly to the pillows and sheets. Any self-consciousness I had at this point disappeared. I felt I was slowly losing my mind. My yearning to explode was all-consuming. With her other hand, Sophie grabbed the front of my neck and grasped firmly. Being slightly choked only heightened the sensation and brought me up even higher, sending an electric shock through my body.

The explosion overcame me from within, as I let out a loud cry, experiencing the most intense orgasm I've ever had in my life. I held it, suspended for almost 10 seconds, until I came down, pushing myself down deeper on Jack's dick. He and Sophie managed to make me come and surge with wetness that released itself almost as violently as a man does when he comes.

There remained a tingling sensation, and my pussy was throbbing as I felt my orgasm leave my body. Jack kissed the back of my neck, withdrew his dick from inside me slowly, and I let out a small moan as even that sensation tickled my insides. I fell on top of Sophie and he fell to her side. In the moments after, my body was quivering slightly to recover. She kissed me, and we smiled as we kissed each other.

"Your heart is beating so fast," she said. I kissed her neck, and then moved down her body, taking each pink nipple in my mouth, sucking gently. As I looked up, she closed her eyes and laid her head back, relishing my tongue and mouth on her tits.

Jack began stroking himself as he watched me and Sophie together.

I continued moving down her body, kissing and sucking on her gorgeous creamy skin. I nibbled at the edge of her belly button, got to the top of her pubic bone, and, with my hands spread her legs apart and bent my head near her pussy. She was waxed bare and already wet from her own touch. I started at her clitoris, the tiny ball above her mauve-colored pussy lips, which darkened where they converged toward the middle. It looked symmetric, pretty, and neat and made me wonder if mine looked this beautiful close-up.

I lowered my head and put my mouth on her clit.

"Oh," she let out, quietly, with a breath.

I lapped my tongue on her clit, slowly, up and down, and then circled around. I continued and felt her hips moving along to my rhythm.

"Mmmmm," I said, slightly muffled. I then went lower, wanting to taste her in my mouth. I let my tongue penetrate the middle of her folds, lapping inside of her. She tasted slightly salty and tangy, and I liked how she tasted, so I continued to reach my tongue deeper in her, back and forth in a slow rhythm. As I looked up, Sophie's eyes were closed and her hands were gripping the sheets on each side beside of her. Jack was on his back and looking at the two of us, still stroking himself slowly.

I moved up and placed my mouth on her clit, applying more pressure and licking her with small short laps.

"Ohhhhh," she said, as her hips contorted from my tongue. I slipped the tips of my thumb and index fingers inside her, gently stroking her as I kept licking her clit.

I reached my left hand out and cupped her breast, taking her nipple in my fingertips and squeezing gently, which made her squirm. I continued lapping at her with my wet mouth, up and down, harder, slower.

Her back suddenly arched up, and she began small thrusts with her hips into my fingers. I continued licking her in my slow rhythm. I felt her hips go faster and faster into my fingers and I kept my mouth locked on the top of her pussy.

"Oh, I'm going to come," she said breathlessly. Then, her body stayed still at first, and then shook as she let out a loud cry mid-air, as her body suspended itself briefly and then fell back down to the bed.

I removed my mouth and gave her pussy a couple of gentle kisses. As I removed my fingers, I saw that they were dripping with her wetness. I laid on my back between Sophie and Jack, and Sophie and I giggled as we watched Jack stroke himself harder and harder, and just as he was about to come, he rolled over on top of me, spread my legs, and penetrated deep inside me again, this time filling me up with his come as he moaned and let out a deep groan.

Afterward, we lay there for about half an hour, the three of us, staring at the ceiling, smoking, cuddling, massaging each other, and half making out.

Jack got up, looked at me, grinned, and said, "I guess we should be going now." And with that, we gathered our clothes from being strewn about on the floor. Sophie stretched out in her bed, smiling as she watched us. When we were ready to leave, I didn't want her to get up, but she did anyway, wrapping herself up in the white hotel robe.

She said she wanted to stay in touch, and handed me her phone so I could add my contact details. I added my first name only, and the email address I usually use for junk mail subscriptions.

At the door, I gave her a last kiss on the lips and said a quick, soft "Bye," as Jack took my hand and led me out into the hallway. Before turning the corner at the end of the hall, I smiled to myself and craned my head back for one last look. The hallway was quiet and dark, and the "Do Not Disturb" sign was hanging on her door.

Did you enjoy *The First Time*?
If so, please rate and review it on
Goodreads and Amazon

★ ★ ★ ★ ★

Thank you! Your readership is **everything**.

About the Author

Shindy Chen manages a weekly variety blog on her site shindychen.com, and is a regular contributor to The Huffington Post. She writes about technology, fashion, luxury travel, personal finance, and lifestyle and career tips. She is the founder of Scribe, a content consultancy and publisher. Her first book, "The Credit Cleanup Book," was published by Praeger in 2014. This is her first work of erotic fiction.

Connect with the Author

You can connect with me across all of my social media channels.

Facebook: shindychenwrites
Instagram: @shindychen
Twitter: @shindychen
Snapchat: realshindychen

Publisher contact: tft@thescri.be

Acknowledgements

Approximately two years ago, on a whim, I thought it'd be fun to write erotica. And when people asked, "Why erotica?" I thought, "Why not?"

In fact, it was at end of the release party for my first (and decidedly un-erotic, personal finance) book, where I stood upon a footstool, announced that my next project would be erotica, and then promptly told everyone in the room that they didn't have to go home, but they had to get the fuck outta there. I'd had a couple of vodka mules in my system by this point.

Fast forward two years and you have in your hands the product of that announcement.

Special thanks to Katie Salisbury for being the most skilled and insightful publishing editor in all the land. She is wise beyond her years and I always learn something from her every time we speak. Thank you Snow Marie Reese for the final proofread and eagle-eye editing work.

Thanks to Francisco Reynoso for designing my awesome book cover. I blabbed about my vision and gave you a hand-drawn scribble, and you made it into beauté.

A huge thanks to those who took their time to

read and provide feedback on the earliest drafts: Jeff (extra thanks for helping me clear those mental blocks), Jasmin, Schuanne, Katie K., and Harsha.

My gratitude also goes to my dear friends and colleagues who lent their words of support—too many to name, you know who you are.

Thanks to my parents and family for supporting me, always. To F. for his loving support and just *being*.

Finally, thank you to all my readers, fans, and followers who picked up a copy of "The First Time." I truly appreciate it—your readership truly means the world to me!